Desert Moms

Written and Illustrated
By
Sharon Ann Burton

This book is printed on acid free paper.
Printed in the United States of America

First published by Dog Ear Publishing
4011 Vincennes Road
Indianapolis, IN 46268
www.dogearpublishing.net

ISBN: 978-1-4575-4375-3

This book is
dedicated to my beautiful
granddaughter, who is always
an inspiration to me.

I love you very much...
Grammy

I ♡ LoVe Books

This book belongs to

Hou Saina

This is the southwestern desert, where the sun is bright and shines down on many animal mothers and their babies. Foxes live in dens and the babies are called kits.

Sharon Ann Barton

Can you help the mother fox find her kits playing the game of Hide and Seek? What kind of plants are they hiding behind?

This is a bobcat mother and her babies. They climb the trees in the southwestern desert, where the sun shines brightly.

Sharon Ann Burton

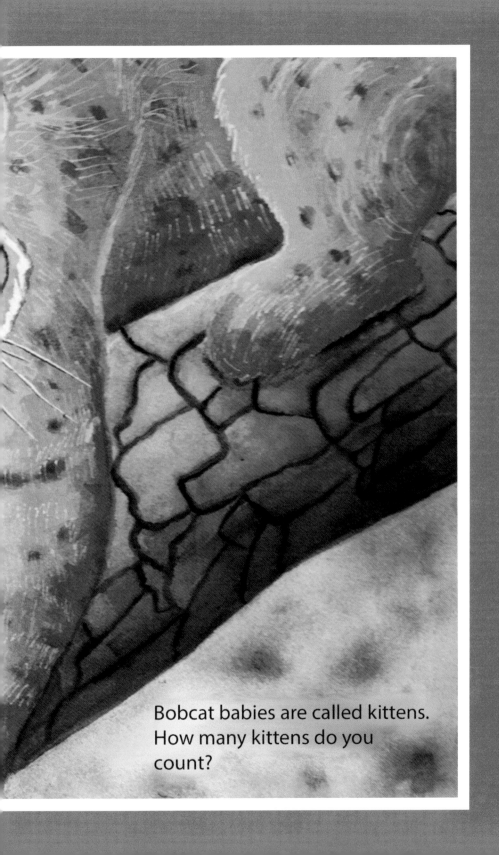

Bobcat babies are called kittens. How many kittens do you count?

This is a javelina (hah-vuh-lee-nuh) mother and her babies. They live in the southwestern desert. The babies are called "reds" because that color can be seen in their bristly hair.

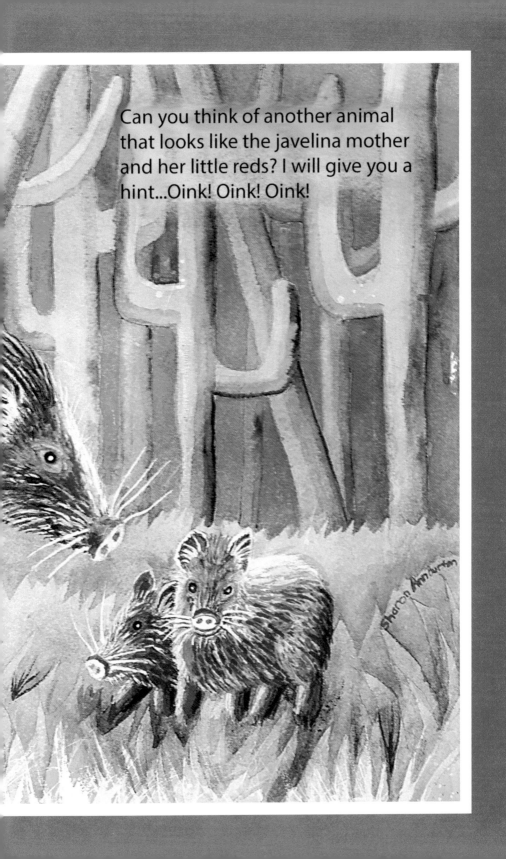

Can you think of another animal that looks like the javelina mother and her little reds? I will give you a hint...Oink! Oink! Oink!

In the southwestern desert we find beautiful prickly pear cactus and a mother white-tailed deer snuggling with her little babies. The mother is known as a doe and the babies are called fawns. Can you spot what the babies have on their fur that they will lose when they get older?

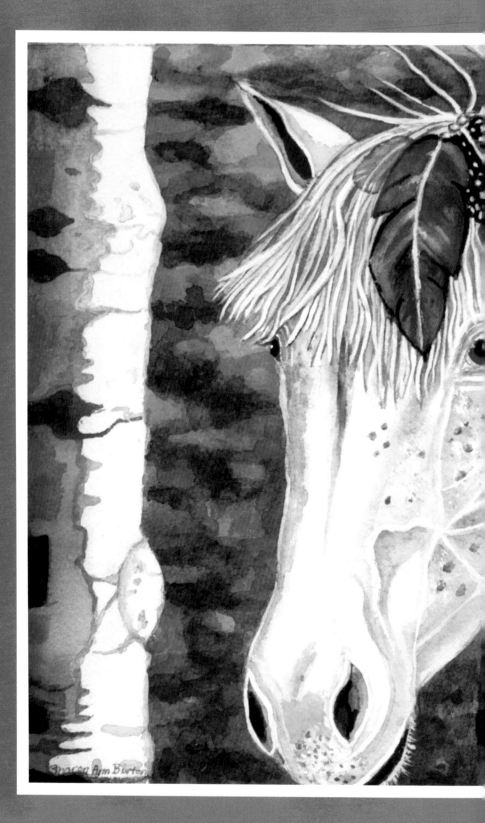

Wild horses and their babies still roam through trees and spiny shrubs in the southwestern desert. Mothers are called mares and their babies are called foals. A mare can have up to two babies. What do you see on the mother's head and back?

In the southwestern desert the sun shines brightly on the top of a house where a mother raven can be seen with her small babies. The raven looks like a crow but is much bigger. It is almost the size of a hawk and very smart. Baby ravens are called nestlings or chicks. Can you guess what part of the house these babies are perching or standing on with their mother? Here is a hint...it is really, really high up!

In the southwestern desert the sun shines brightly on the mountains and hills lined with giant saguaro (suh-wahr-oh) cactus plants. A mother roadrunner can be seen feeding her babies. The roadrunner is a bird that hardly ever flies but can run very fast. The babies are called nestlings, hatchlings or chicks. Do you know what the little chicks are eating? Do you think it is yummy or yucky?

In the southwestern desert the sun shines brightly on the giant saguaro cactus plant with its beautiful white flowers. A tiny mother elf owl is on one of its branches while her babies are cuddling together in a hole in the cactus trunk. These owls are nocturnal so they hunt for food at night and sleep during the daytime. Can you count the number of white flowers that are on the branches of the saguaro cactus plant?

A mother prairie dog and her babies have come out of their burrow or hole below the ground in the southwestern desert. They have this name because they make sounds like a barking dog. The babies are called pups. What are these prairie dogs doing that always feels so good?

In the southwestern desert we find a mother ringtail cat and her babies. They are related to the racoon. They are nocturnal animals. Remember this means they like to move about at night to look for food. The babies are called cubs. How is the mother ringtail carrying her cubs? What do they have on their tails? Here is a hint...it is in their name.

Sharon Ann Burton

In the southwestern desert the moon shines brightly on a mother coyote and her babies. Her babies are called cubs.

They are famous for their nightly howling or singing to each other. Can you make a howling sound like the coyote? Let's try together!

These are some of the beautiful animals that live in the southwestern desert, where the sun is bright and shines down on the mothers taking care of their lovely little babies, like all moms do.